The Misfit Christmas Puddings

Club Consolation

THE MISFIT CHRISTMAS PUDDINGS

First Episode

HERR BAUMGÄRTNER'S ESTABLISHMENT EIGHT O'CLOCK IN THE MORNING THE DAY BEFORE CHRISTMAS

IT WAS the day before Christmas, yet there was no need to tell that to any one in Buffalo, for everywhere in the city was the stir and excitement that precedes a great holiday. Every one seemed to be alert and in a hurry. The very air was full of Christmas scents. One felt that something unusual was going on, and nowhere was this more apparent than in Baker Baumgärtner's large establishment.

Among the German residents of this prosperous lake port this was the most popular bakery in the town, and Herr Baumgärtner was caterer and confectioner as well as baker. Consequently he had a very large trade, and the twelve wagons that were despatched daily from the Baumgärtner bakery went to all parts of the city. Not only was he popular among the German residents, but whoever had once tasted the baker's crisp rolls and genuine German rye bread—not to mention the Lebkuchen and Pfeffernüsse at Christmastime—never neglected an opportunity to order more. Even the delicious Marzipan Brod—a sweetmeat made of almonds, sugar, and rose-water—was not omitted from his Christmas confections. Certainly, Herr Baumgärtner's establishment was almost too tempting for one who possessed but a slender pocketbook at Christmas-time.

The windows, washed and polished until they fairly shone, were now hung with wreaths of holly, and festoons of evergreens were draped across both doors and windows in token of the holiday season. Two large firtrees in boxes stood on each side of the entrance.

Herr Baumgärtner's Christmas windows were the great delight of all the children in the neighborhood, for in one stood a tall Christmas tree from whose branches dangled the most wonderful candies and cakes,—boys and girls, kings and queens, cows, dogs, funny fat pigs, violins, real Swiss houses,—in fact all kinds of toys. These were made either of chocolate, sugar, or gingerbread. This marvellous tree was also adorned with a huge silver star at the top, while glittering gold and silver paper chains were suspended from its branches. These, and the many colored candles, made it a bewildering sight. Truly, it was a real fairy Christmas tree.

Perhaps no one but Herr Baumgärtner himself knew that this tree was in memory of a little boy who long years before had spent a few short Christmas days with him, for Herr Baumgärtner's only son had died when three years old. The baker was not a man who was supposed to have much sentiment, but he would as soon omit the baking of the Christmas cakes as omit the Christmas tree in remembrance of little Fritz. It certainly was a joy and delight to all the children round about, and so great was its fame that many a child begged "to go just once"—if he lived a long way off—and see the Baumgärtner's wonderful Christmas tree.

Though it was yet early in the morning the wagons were already returning from the delivery of the breakfast rolls and bread. The air of the store was odorous with appetizing scents, attesting the baker's concocting skill. The shelves were filled with fragrant fresh bread, and there was an extra supply of cakes and buns.

Under the glass cases were arranged the most tempting holiday cakes. Particularly attractive was the Lebkuchen,—a highly spiced gingerbread,—which was artistically made into different shapes, some square, others large and round, while again others were in the form of hearts with an ornament of sugar-work around the outside. On many were the words, "Merry Christmas," in tiny red and white candies. The animals made of gingerbread were as numerous as those that went into the Ark. These were done over with a thin white icing, and not a child that entered the bakery could be induced to leave without at least one animal which he selected as his fancy prompted him, while many almost wept because they could not buy all. But perhaps for "grown-ups" the favorite cakes were the hard little Pfeffernüsse.

Large wreaths of pine were suspended from the ceiling, and a feeling of homesickness came over many a German customer at the smell of the favorite Lebkuchen and the words, "Fröhliche Weihnachten,"—for Baker Baumgärtner was a shrewd man and wished his customers a merry

Christmas in German as well as in English, — and they thought of the joyful times in the Fatherland when the Christ-child had visited the home and had brought them just such simple gifts as these.

Baker Baumgärtner was a big, burly man with a loud, gruff voice. He expected prompt obedience from all his employees, — apprentice boys, bakers, and clerks alike, — and this he usually obtained. He was very methodical, attending to every detail of his large business and knowing just what to require from every one under him.

"Be fair and honest" was his motto; yet he delighted in "making moneys," — as he expressed it, — but honestly.

His interests in life seemed to be divided between his growing business and his pretty daughter, Katrina. She was the idol of his eye and he could refuse her nothing, though counted close in business matters.

It was eight o'clock in the morning and trade was beginning briskly. The telephone orders kept the bell jingling. The clerks and bakers were prepared for a busy day, and had received from Herr Baumgärtner their special instructions in regard to the catering and delivering. Already early customers were beginning to come in.

Herr Baumgärtner stood near a table which was in the rear of the store. On this table were displayed thirteen Christmas puddings, set apart in royal aloofness. These the baker intended as presents to some of his best customers.

"Ach, dose puddings!" he soliloquized. "Goot, rich, schön! But I get my moneys back again." In other words, he anticipated a large return from a small investment.

Baker Baumgärtner knew how to do the handsome thing upon occasion, and was possessed of a generosity which, like Bob Acres' courage, "came and went." Just now it was at full tide. Desirous of presenting his gifts in the best possible manner, he went to his desk, and taking out thirteen gilt-edged cards, he wrote on each: "With the Christmas Greetings of Herr Wilhelm Baumgärtner." He next took from its wrapping a quantity of pink and blue tissue paper with embroidered edges.

At this moment Hans Kleinhardt, his head clerk, entered the store.

"Hans, come you here once!" cried the baker. "Dot fine puddings vat you see dere are for my thirteen best customers. Vat you tink, Hans," — showing him the tissue papers, "joost de ting to wrap dot puddings in, nicht wahr? Always in Hirschberg dey say to me, 'Ach, Herr Baumgärtner, Sie haben immer so schönes Papier.'"

"Ja, ja," assented Hans, "it is so fine already."

So anxious was our Hans to ingratiate himself and make a good impression, — for Hans was ambitious, — that had Herr Baumgärtner wished them wrapped in circus posters Hans would have said: "Ja, ja, it is so fine already."

"Dot pink, Hans, ist ausgezeichnet, dot will we haf, and moreover on each tie you a piece of dat Christmas holly mit de red berries. Hans, see. Here is dat list of mein thirteen best customers. Send you dem dose puddings. Each and efery pudding is joost quite alike. Here are dose cardts mit vich I send dem my Christmas Greetings. You see dot dose puddings get sent dis Christmas eve."

Hans put the list and the thirteen cards into his pocket and promised to attend to the order faithfully.

"A 'phone call for you, sir," said one of his clerks.

Herr Baumgärtner went slowly to the telephone. Nothing ever made the good baker hurry, for haste was not in his make-up.

"Hello, vat you vant?"

A large order had not been delivered. That was an unpardonable offence in the Baumgärtner establishment. The baker was slow to be aroused, but when once his anger was awakened he was, indeed, a furious man. The wild, fierce Teuton in him got the upper hand.

"Donner Wetter!" he cried. "Vat for dat big order not delivered, and vone of mein goot customers dat leaves me much moneys? You tink I hire you for noddings, eh? Joost to trow my moneys away on you?"

He stormed and raged at the unlucky clerk through whose carelessness the mistake had occurred.

"Himmel!" he yelled. "How come dat you forget? You are one Dummkopf! I haf not served in die German army for noddings, and ven I say 'You delifer dose tings on Monday' I mean on Monday, and not on Tuesday. You hear dat now?"

The unhappy clerk acknowledged that he heard, and, fortunately for him, the entrance of a wealthy customer saved him from further wrath. The sincere admiration expressed by the customer for the Christmas decorations and the Christmas confections was appreciated by the baker, and the pleasant words, being supplemented by a large order, restored Herr Baumgärtner to his usual good humor. As he returned to his office he could not refrain from pausing a moment beside the table which held the Christmas puddings.

"Ach, dose puddings!" he commented, viewing them with professional pride, "Dey are joost like von picture!"

Second Episode

WIDOW M'CARTY'S ABODE MORNING OF THE DAY BEFORE CHRISTMAS

DOWN on the tow-path was a little, weather-beaten shanty that presented a far different setting for the enactments of the coming holiday.

Here, for six sad months, the Widow M'Carty had tried to keep the wolf from the door, but work as she might, her efforts would hardly have frightened an able-bodied weasel.

It was now some eight months since Michael M'Carty, broad-shouldered, courageous, and loving, had rushed home to his snug cottage one noon-time with the news that he had shipped as assistant engineer on the big, new freighter, the Go-Between, which was to leave port that very night.

Bridget, his wife, had smiled bravely at him through tears that the prospect of separation called to her eyes, but went thriftily to work to get his clothes in readiness; "Fer," said she, "there'll be no tellin' whin they'll feel a needle again."

Michael M'Carty had followed the lakes before, and now with better wages than ever it was no time for "complainin'." Indeed, there never had been any time for "complainin'" in Bridget's cheery, helpful life. Even the maternal cares which had multiplied so rapidly had not robbed her of her girlish buoyancy, and the ninth little M'Carty, at that moment enjoying her father's parting fondling, had been just as welcome as the first, now a proud member of the highest "Grammar Grade," though barely thirteen.

Michael M'Carty was ambitious for his children, and even dreamed of sending his cleverest offspring to the New High School which he passed each morning on his way to work. That presumptuous plan never had been whispered to any one save his "darlin' Biddy," and they dreaded the day when it should be made known to Granny M'Carty, whose presence at the family hearthstone supplied all the discipline that could possibly be needed in any fairly moral household. Granny M'Carty's rule was like unto that of the Chinese mother-in-law, and if anything ever had pleased her since her son brought her to his hospitable home, she had betrayed no suspicion of the feeling.

On the occasion described Granny swayed to and fro in her chair,—the most comfortable that the house afforded,—and wailed:

"Ochone, sorra the day! The banshee was singin' onunder the windy last night, an' ye'll be drownded, sure; or failin' or that ye won't know onny more than to go ashore at Chicagy an' there ye'll be murthered to death with one of them hand-bags, worra, worra!"

If the demon of pessimism lurked by the M'Carty fireside in the person of Granny M'Carty, that malign influence was offset by the angel of optimism who brooded over the family circle under the name of Grandad Rafferty.

Grandad, whose society was the only dowry that Bridget Rafferty had brought to her husband, now interposed his sweet, quavering tones.

"Whist, Granny, don't be undoin' the b'y jist as he's leavin' Biddy an' the childer. The blessid Virgin will fetch him back all right. Good luck to ye, lad. Ye're a fine son to me, an' I'll mind Biddy an' the chicks an' look after them while ye are away."

Grandad was right. He certainly would "mind" the children, for their lightest word was law to him. He would "look after" them, and fondly, too, but his feeble limbs never could follow the antics of the merry little brood.

With a varied cargo of good wishes and gloomy forebodings, and with Bridget's gold ring on his finger "for luck," Michael steamed away,— sorrowful at leaving his dear ones, but glad that fortune favored his honest efforts for their comfortable support.

Never had such a storm swept the lakes in spring-time as buffeted the poor Go-Between, yet untried by wind and wave. Unskilful loading interfered with a perfect ballast, and unseamanlike management left her at the mercy of the tempest.

"WENT DOWN WITH ALL ON BOARD!"

was the head-line that greeted faithful Bridget M'Carty on the morning of that dreadful day a week after Michael had left her, and before she could snatch a paper her heart told her the name of the boat.

Though a tireless worker, Bridget had always depended upon Michael for the management of their small affairs, and at first she was bewildered by the responsibility thrust upon her. It took time to recover from the shock of the sad news and to make plans and find work that would put bread into twelve hungry mouths. In that time the little store of savings was expended, for in addition to all the other troubles, Granny M'Carty brooded herself ill, and the doctor's bill had to be paid.

It was soon apparent that the snug little home in which Michael had left his family must be abandoned for humbler quarters. Inexperienced in house-hunting and feeling restricted to the lowest possible rent, Mrs. M'Carty fell a prey to an unprincipled landlord, who induced her to take her flock to a ramshackle abode on the tow-path which he described as "quite habitable."

The place had not seemed so objectionable while warm weather lasted. The passing canal-boats with their patient motive power afforded unfailing interest to the little M'Cartys by day, and the swish of the displaced waters lulled them to sleep at night.

Viewed objectively, the place perhaps was not without attractions. "A real live painter" had once pitched his easel near at hand, causing a little M'Carty to run home breathless with the information that he had called their house "picturesque."

When Grandad Rafferty heard this compliment to their domicile, he said, — "Picteresk is it? Well, that is a comfort!" But Granny M'Carty refused to be deceived by empty words; "Picteresk, indade! Let them live on that who can!"

Half-covered with snow in the freezing winter weather, the picturesque element of the M'Carty home was lost in desolation, and on this December day even stout-hearted Bridget was obliged to let her feelings partake of the prevailing atmosphere.

Salt tears trickled down the poor woman's cheeks and fell into the tub where she was "doin' out" the wash of some street-car conductors not fortunate enough to have womenfolk of their own.

"Indeed," said Bridget with doleful humor, "that's all the salt water these poor shirts will be getting to set their color, and oh, dear! I wish they were Michael's."

She sank down on an upturned tub and gave way to her bitter grief as she seldom allowed herself to do.

"Sure, it's the first Christmas since my name was M'Carty that the tub will be upside down. The childer couldn't always spare a stocking apiece for hanging up, but it was many a bit they found in the tub. My pie, Mike used to be calling it.

"And now it's him that is dead, and we've not even a meal in the pantry — no, nor pantry neither, and what'll become of us now?"

But Mrs. M'Carty soon realized that even the luxury of time to mourn was denied the poor, and she controlled herself resolutely with the words:

"There, ain't ye ashamed of yourself, Biddy M'Carty? As if it were not bad enough to have the trouble in your heart without grieving about it aloud into the bargain. Supposing the children were all dead, and Grandad were blind, and — and Granny were took away, and yourself were in the insane crazy asylum. Then would be time to be wasting in weeping."

So, leaving tears for the pastime of lunatics, Bridget bravely furbished up her philosophy and brought it into use.

To make up for lost time she applied herself to the shirts with such vigor that the very fabric was in danger of disappearing with the spots of dirt which she attacked. These garments must be ready as soon as possible, for she needed the money to which their cleansing entitled her.

She had just sent Katy and Norah out with her last piece of work. It was not lucrative, being the washing for the little lame seamstress who could not afford to pay much, but for whom Mrs. M'Carty, with the generosity of the warm-hearted Irish, continued to work.

The family income was somewhat augmented by the willing efforts of Dennis and Terence, and they were now absent in the pursuit of their vocation, the sale of daily newspapers.

Mary and Maggie, too young to be of assistance, were quietly dressing up Granny's stick in a bit of tattered shawl and playing that it was a witch, at any moment liable to pounce on Granny and carry her off, the wish, perhaps, being father to the thought. Unobserved, the little girls were making threatening gestures behind the old lady's chair, indicative of her impending fate. Meantime they cast fearful glances toward the owner of the stick, the danger of momentary discovery adding pleasurable excitement to their pastime.

Baby Ellen was asleep in her favorite resting-place, Grandad's arms. The two younger boys were making themselves unpopular by toddling back and forth between the living-room and the lean-to, from which latter place came the dull rhythm of Mrs. M'Carty's scrub, scrub, scrub on the washboard.

An outbreak from Granny heralded the interruption of the witch drama, and brought Bridget to the spot. The children were dodging behind Grandad's chair, while Granny poured the vials of her wrath on their offending heads, at the same time indulging in her favorite custom of throwing at them the articles within her reach. Perhaps the one compensation in the paucity of the furnishings of the M'Carty home was the limitation on the vehicles of Granny's wrath.

"Och, them spalpeens!" she shouted as her daughter-in-law entered, "bad 'cess to them, rampin' an' rampagin' 'round till me ears is jist burshtin'!"

Mrs. M'Carty, feeling that some one ought to be punished, and not thinking it quite filial to belabor her mother-in-law, caught up two or three of her olive branches that were recklessly waving in the air, and imprinted on them a few gentle reminders of maternal solicitude. Howls rent the air, but these were largely for effect, for Bridget had a whole-souled way with her in administering punishment, which left no lasting resentment in the objects of her discipline.

Always concerned lest the correction of her grandchildren be lacking in severity, Granny growled:

"Sthop yer whillelewin' an' phillelewin'! Ye ought to have a strap, so ye had!"

She felt a certain satisfaction in the crisis which she had precipitated, but it did not temper her speech, for as soon as the children were quiet she broke forth.

"Begorra, perhaps it's a nice Christmas we'll be havin' with the winter here with its searchin' cold, an' nothin' but this shanty with its two rooms an' lean-to, an' half the furnitoor gone to pay rent, an' put food in the mouths of that greedy raft of childer. An' jist feel my roomatiz!" her voice growing more shrill with excitement, "an' not a whole pane in the windy, but it's many a pain I have in me bones. An' I nade linnyment this minit. An' look at him settin' there," pointing wrathfully at Grandad Rafferty, "an' not makin' anybody trouble!" and she paused as if to contemplate the pleasure that would be afforded her to see Grandad making somebody a great deal of trouble.

"An' there's my poor Michael," she went on, "drownded an the wather an' wearin' that nice gold ring on his skellington."

"Oh, don't," moaned poor Bridget, putting up her hand as if to ward off the blow of cruel words. But Granny, finding her ravings were making an impression, grew more fluent.

"I don't doubt me there was the price of a bottle of linnyment in that ring, an' more, an' ye that extravagant to be makin' him wear it when ye knew he'd be drowned."

Bridget and Grandad were at their wit's end, as many a time before, for words with which to soothe the old woman. Though he inwardly resented this abuse of his daughter, Grandad tried as usual to pour oil on the seething waters.

"Annyhow, Granny, it's a mercy it was a real gold ring, an' not one of them chape things to be gettin' all rusty in the wather."

Granny flew into a more violent rage.

"An' are ye insinooatin', Misther Rafferty, that my son would ever wear an old brass ring? I'd have ye know that real gold is none too good for the poor, dear b'y to be drownded in. An' I wish ye'd stop yer talkin', ye blatherin' omadhaun," she snapped out, and then relapsed into sullen silence, setting her empty pipe upside down in her mouth, a veritable picture of despair.

But Granny's silence, even, could make itself felt. Grandad was speechless. Dear old Grandad! The sun of his cheerfulness had suffered no eclipse from the clouds of adversity that enveloped the M'Carty family. His "Marnin', honey!" and "Avenin', shure!" sounded as pleasantly as ever. When he had bread he ate it thankfully, and when there was none he said that his "sthomick had a sort of full feelin' of itsilf."

He was a constant comfort to his daughter, but the sweetness of his spirit was gall and wormwood to Granny. If there is one thing more exasperating than another to a caustic temperament, it is the constant companionship of a bland and optimistic disposition. In Granny's case the necessity of maintaining both sides of a quarrel kept her tongue sharpened to a piercing point.

After a moment's quiet, Mrs. M'Carty slipped the pipe out of Granny's mouth and returned it to her filled. It was accepted, though thanklessly. With a smile and an understanding nod to her father, Bridget returned to her tubs.

She finished her washing and put things to rights. Then she drew from a box where she kept a few things from Granny's prying eyes, her sorry Christmas presents,—some pictures cut from an illustrated paper and pasted on squares of cardboard.

"The poor darlings," she said. "I can't even be buying them trifling presents. I must be saving every penny, for the first of the month is coming, and the agent, bad 'cess to him, will be here to lift the rent. An' these poor picters is all I've got for Christmas for the biggest ones, and nothing at all for the next size, and the same for the middlest size and the littlest ones, and never a thing for the baby. I most wish I'd let little Patsy keep the ball he stole from the Wilkeson boy."

The strain of the recent encounter had told on Mrs. M'Carty's usually steady nerves, and her inability to contribute to her children's holiday enjoyment filled her with sudden resentment.

"I suppose them Barneys up on Fifth Street will every one of them be strutting and ballyragging 'round with gewgaws, and fixings, and such like things. Faith, they'll need them to be making themselves look decent, so they will. Truth, every single one of them Barneys has more freckles than I could find on my whole nine together, if I searched with a candle. And why can't they be having what they're after wanting! Anybody can buy that has money."

Bridget laid the pictures back in the box.

"You can stay there," she said, closing the cover. "It will never do to be giving something to one and nothing to the rest of them. Bedad, I'd like to put my eye on a dollar once. It's always to be watching a cent that makes a body short-sighted."

Third Episode

HERR BAUMGÄRTNER'S ESTABLISHMENT TEN O'CLOCK IN THE MORNING THE DAY BEFORE CHRISTMAS

IT was Herr Baumgärtner's habit to open his mouth almost as prudently as his purse, but when at ten o'clock one of his clerks returned without the amount of the bill he had been sent out to collect, the baker lost patience.

"You cannot get dat moneys! Haf you said how I must pay my insurance, and all der clerks in dis big store, and all der extras for Christmas? How will I pay for dem if my moneys comes not back again? Haf you said how I must haf it?"

The clerk explained that he had told Mr. Weiss, the debtor, all this and that he had said he would pay, without fail, the first of the next month.

"Next mont'!" cried the indignant baker. "He haf told me dat same t'ing six times already! First he write he will send it next mont'; den he say, 'Soon as my interest is due I will pay;' next times, 'My wife she is sick and you must wait yet a little while.' Go tell him I vill haf dat moneys dis day!"

The clerk departed as he was bidden. The baker shook his head angrily.

"Ach, dose peoples! I haf no patience mit dem. In Germany Fritz Weiss was dat honest and goot. It is all along of his wife. She must haf one fine house, and dere girls such clot'es,—like one Baronin,—vich is bad for dem, and for my Katrina too, ven she know of it. Bewahre, dat my Katrina should so dress. Yet I haf die means and Fritz he haf not. So foolish a wife he haf. Gott sei Dank! My blessed wife war nicht so. She had always so much goot sense, and dose girls are not like my Katrina. Nein, I haf not seen one Mädchen like mein Katrina, immer sehr schön und gut."

At this moment Herr Baumgärtner looked out of his office and saw his Katrina entering the store.

"Ach, dere is mein Katrina. She makes me always glad ven I see her," he mused, watching her with loving eyes as she came through the store.

Katrina was a picture to delight other eyes than those of her father. A mass of wavy, flaxen hair framed a face of rare tints of pink and pearl. Beautiful blue eyes she had, eyes that could be trustful or merry under their long lashes, while the sweet, smiling mouth with its full-arched upper lip was not the least of Katrina's charms. When one looked at her it was like beholding the vision of some bewitching, Saxon princess.

Herr Baumgärtner was not burdened with a large family, for he had only this one daughter, so it would seem that Katrina Baumgärtner might have advantages denied many of her companions. She had rather unusual advantages, for while her girl friends were learning to paint uncertain flowers, and to entertain with equally dubious musical accomplishments, Katrina's father had insisted that his daughter must learn the art of the housewife.

As Katrina passed through the store she had a word or a nod of recognition for each busy clerk, and for the customers whom she knew. She stopped to leave a small package with Max Schaub for his little lame August; and when George Reigel's sick Freda opened her box on Christmas morning she was to find a doll that Miss Katrina's artful fingers had dressed.

When Katrina's mother was alive she had taught her child, through years of precept and example, an uncommon interpretation of the holiday giving, — that the family and friends were not to be thought of until many a Christmas surprise had been planned for the needy and unexpectant. The baker himself came in for a share of the waves of gratitude that swept toward his home at each holiday season, though this tide of good feeling was largely due to his thoughtful daughter.

Katrina felt the blessedness of giving, but just now she had other joys, as well, to keep her heart aglow. She was at the age when most girls have considerable liberty in their personal affairs, but this was not the case with Katrina.

Herr Baumgärtner settled the questions of his household with the same attention and decision that he gave to his business. Consequently his daughter was a frequent visitor at her father's store, where she came to consult him on the trivial as well as upon the most important questions pertaining to their domestic concerns.

When she presented herself before Herr Baumgärtner's desk on this morning before Christmas, he greeted her with his usual question on such occasions:

"Was willst du, Katrinchen?"

"Something nice this time, Vater. The big snow-storm has come just in time for Christmas, you know, and I am invited to a sleigh-ride party to-night. I may go, may I not?"

"A sleigh-ride den?" and he smiled and said, "Only once is one young!— But who asked you to go on dat sleigh-ride?"

"Johann Hermann asked me this morning," replied Katrina, blushing a little, "but I told him I must first ask you."

"Ach, so! Vat for a man is der Johann dat of a morning he comes to ask you, Tochterchen? Vat does he?"

"He keeps books, Father, and he stopped on his way to his work. He came just after you had gone this morning, and he will come at noon to see if I may go."

"Is he son of dat Herr Frederick Hermann dat knows not so much to stick to one job steady?"

"Oh, no, Father, he is not like that," protested Katrina, earnestly. "He told me this morning that he meant to work hard while he was young so that he might earn money enough to be able to rest when he is old. He said he knew a man who had made a bank account that way, and he meant to do it too."

"Nun, gut,—dat man he means might be me, Katrina," said Herr Baumgärtner, with a little glance of pride at his inner man.

"He did not say it was you, Vater, but he is a good young man and I know you will like him. And I may go?"

Herr Baumgärtner found it very hard to refuse Katrina anything, and when he felt obliged to do so he consoled himself with the reflection:

"It causes me sorrow not to give her everyt'ings, but it is better for her."

However, he felt that this was not the time for the discipline of self-denial, so he gave his consent.

"Ja wohl, to-night kannst du, Katrinchen."

"Oh, thank you, thank you, Father," and she gave his arm an affectionate squeeze as together they passed out of the office.

"Doesn't the store look fine, and how good everything smells," said Katrina, delighting in the spicy odors. But Katrina was in a mood to be delighted with anything.

"So much thoughts, so great work, das ist," replied her father, looking at the exemplification of the law of supply and demand going on steadily before them, and added, "but die trade goes well dis year."

"That is good, and when all is sold to-night that will be sold before the Christmas you will not forget the cakes and goodies for my poor little ones for to-morrow, will you? I have some of my Christmas money saved to pay for them, but I must have a great many for my money, five times as much as I could get with it anywhere else, or I will not buy here any more, Herr Papa," said Katrina roguishly.

"Ach, Katrina, vy t'row so goot stuff away on dose children? Dey know not der value. I tell you it is joost one big waste."

Katrina was too wise to argue with her father even if he would have permitted, and she knew that she would get her cakes in spite of his grumbling. Turning she saw the table with its array of Christmas puddings.

"Oh, what beautiful puddings!" she exclaimed. "Would they not make such a handsome window with a bit of Christmas holly on each of them?"

"Ja, so dose puddings would make one splendit window, Liebchen," said the baker. "So much eggs, und raisins, und currants, und spices, und wine dey took, und six hours to cook each one. But dey will keep a year."

"And are they all sold?" asked Katrina.

"Nein, nein, Katrina, we sell not one of dose puddings."

"Not sell them, Father! Are you going to give them away?"

"Katrina, Katrina, you remember not anyt'ings to-day. At home haf I not said how I send out one puddings each to mein best customers, and on die card my compliments?" and Herr Baumgärtner straightened himself proudly.

"Oh, that is so. I had forgotten," said Katrina. "But if I were going to give them away I would not send them to rich people who have money to buy them. I would send them to poor people who never have such treats."

"Katrina, you know not business. You t'ink der fisherman he put dat worm on dat hook to feed der fish, eh? Den how come all dose fish at night in his basket?"

Katrina never let any differences with her father stare her out of countenance, so as he turned toward his office she followed him.

"I nearly forgot one thing I wanted, Father. May I have a cake to send to the Widow M'Carty? She is the woman who washes for us sometimes, you know."

"Lieber Himmel! Vy should I send to the Widow M'Carty one cake? Nein, Katrina. Should I gif everyt'ing away? Vat mit der baskets for dose orphan asylums yet, I am like one big Santa Clauses already."

"But Mrs. M'Carty has nine little children, Vater—"

"Maype she has, I care not. I feed not so many people's nine children."

"Oh, Father, this will be such a sad Christmas for the poor woman. It is not a year, yet, since her husband was drowned. And think of those nine little M'Cartys with no dear, kind, handsome papa like mine,"—Herr Baumgärtner's features relaxed a little,—"and you've often told me when Grossvater Baumgärtner went to Hirschberg with you and the little Hans that died, how that kind man—"

"Dere, dere, Katrina," broke in Herr

Baumgärtner in an unsteady voice. "Take dot cake, and I hope it will not choke dose M'Cartys mit der strangeness of eating anyt'ing so goot."

Fourth Episode

WIDOW M'CARTY'S ABODE SIX O'CLOCK ON CHRISTMAS EVE

DESPITE the many mechanical operations performed upon the family clock by the little M'Cartys, it ticked away the minutes, and the hours, and the days faithfully. Even on this special Christmas Eve when the fortunes of its owners seemed at their very lowest ebb, it did not so much as moderate its voice or slacken its movements. When the hour arrived that its long hand should point straight upward and its short hand straight downward, the bells of the city began to ring, and the whistles of the city began to blow, announcing, with much clamor and discordance, that another day of labor was ended.

At the shriek of the first whistle Grandad Rafferty, who sat by the fire with baby Ellen on his knee, looked up at the clock and nodded to it approvingly.

"Arrah now, ye little leprechaune that works while the rest do be shlapin', ye're tellin' the truth same as ever, for it's time for them that's workin' to be sthoppin'. I mind when I was young an' sphry how glad I was to lave me workin' an' run home to me swate Maggie, God rest her soul! And when she see me comin' over the hill, she'd be steppin' down the lane to mate me. And afther supper I'd smoke me dudheen whilst Maggie redded up the cabin and then—"

"True for ye," broke in Granny M'Carty from her seat on the opposite side of the fire. She could not abide Grandad Rafferty's reminiscences, for they recalled to her the happy days in the old country,—the place to which her heart turned ever with longing, though she never expected to put foot again on its green turf. "It's ye that would sit and smoke an' yer Maggie workin' her legs off slavin' for yez. Och, it's the men have the aisy time in this life, but it's them same, I'm thinkin', that will pay for it by a longer sthop in purgatory, and I hope they will, so I do."

"Indade, now, Mrs. M'Carty," began Grandad Rafferty, soothingly, "sure, the men have—"

"Indade, then, they have not!" contradicted Granny. "Look at them men that's goin' home this minit,"—waving her hand as if toward a procession of laborers passing before her. "What have they to do? In the mornin' they're off with a fine lunch in their pails, an' never a bed to make, or a floor to swape, or a childer to clane, or a male to be cookin'. It's the womin must sthay at home and mind all that. And when they're home at night they'll eat their supper an' likely grumble at it, then sit at their ease an' smoke. Troth, if I had the word—"

"Musha, musha, Mrs. M'Carty!" said Grandad. "Ye're clane forgettin' the men work hard all day, that the womin may sthay safe at home with their jewels of childers."

"Jewels of childers, indade!" exclaimed Granny, her attention turned to a new grievance. "Them kind of jewels poor folks could do well withoot."

"Listen to that now, Ellen, me jewel," said Grandad Rafferty, addressing himself to the baby on his knee. "Listen, but don't ye belave a worrd ye're hearin'. Yer Granny would not part with yez for long money. Would ye, Mrs. M'Carty? An' is she not ev'ry bit as fine a child as yer Michael when he wor a baby?"

"Me Michael—may the Hivens be his bed—had the sense to be born a b'y, an' there was but two of him, an' here's yer grandchilder springin' up like blades of the grass for number. Oh, Michael, Michael," wailed Granny, "if ye could only see yer old mither now, 'tis not aisy ye'd rest in yer grave if ye had a grave, which ye haven't, worse luck. Here I be, with never a dacent bit or sup, me that in the old counthry had bacon with me praties an' a fine shawl fer Sunday," and at this point Granny began to weep.

"Whist now, whist, Granny!" cried Mrs. M'Carty, coming in from the lean-to where she had been to bestow the insignia of her office, her board and tubs. "Don't be grieving with yerself. I'll make the supper an' ye'll feel better when ye have something warm in yer stomick. It's not much we have, but when Dinny and Terence grow a bit more—"

"Grow is it?" exclaimed Granny, finding in Bridget's words another source of wrath. "Ye'd betther be prayin' the saints to kape thim from growin'. Their clothes is far too small fer their size this minit."

"Now Granny, it's yerself knows me prayers won't keep them boys from growing, but it's hoping I am that the clothes will come with their bigness."

"That's like yer foolishness, Bridget M'Carty," retorted Granny. "It's ye that is always expectin' somethin' betther the morrow. It's the worst ye should be lookin' for, so it is, for it's that ye'll be afther gettin', more like."

"Now Granny," replied Mrs. M'Carty, "it's never a minit I'll be wasting getting ready for troubles, for when troubles come they're a different sort entirely than them you do be ready for."

At this moment the door, true to its habit of flying open at any and all times, swung briskly on its hinges, and admitted Denny and Terence returned from their sale of evening papers. Terence carried a small package while Denny waved aloft a branch of evergreen which he had rescued from the street.

"Look every one of you and see what Terence is after bringing," cried Denny.

"Ye've left the door open on me poor old bones," complained Granny.

Five little M'Cartys sprang to shut the door.

"It's samples I have—enough for the whole of us," said Terence, proudly displaying the contents of his bundle. "And it's a bit of milk you put with it and it's cooked. I seen them on the counter when I ran in a grocery to warm my fingers. 'Take one,' the card said, and I asked the clerk an' he says, 'Take two, you'll be a good advertisement for it.'"

"Wheat Krakle, it is," said Denny, taking up one of the samples and reading the label. "Better than meat, and more n-o-u nur, r-i ri, s-h-i-n-g shing, nourishing, whatever that may be. And I says to Terence, 'what's two of them with twelve of us?' and says I, 'let's ask 'round and get one apiece,' and here you have them."

Granny who, before the opening of the package, had hoped it might contain a "bit o' bacon, or a dhrawin' o' tay," of which luxuries she had been deprived for some time, leaned back in her chair with a groan.

"Och hone, it's just one more of them new aitin's to sphile my stomick," she said. "May the devil fly away with them that makes them. Sure along with them haythinish sthuffs I've ate since poor Michael died on us, me insides feel like Brian O'Connell's oatfield in the old counthry, an' that same was half-bog an' half-bushes, bad scran to it!"

"Now then, Mrs. M'Carty," said Grandad Rafferty, as usual finding some good in everything, "have ye no thought how ye're savin' yer teeth with these new aitin's that shlip down so aisy ye're not to the throuble of chewin' them?"

But Granny was not to be mollified, and she refused to sit down with either of the relays of the family which gathered at the tiny table and partook of the food that was "Better than meat and far more nourishing."

Supper being over and the dishes hastily washed by Katy, the four elder M'Cartys were allowed to set forth for an evening walk to admire the festive preparations for the morrow's holiday,—a holiday in the pleasures of which they had no hope of sharing. Four more M'Cartys were despatched to their humble couches, two of them, owing to Granny's faultfinding, having been spanked vigorously before being turned over to the arms of Morpheus. After all, perhaps the latter pair were the ones to be envied, as the heat thus engendered made the scantiness of the bedding less apparent.

Granny M'Carty in the easiest chair and Grandad Rafferty in the next easiest, sat in silence on either side of the little stove that did double duty as heater and cooker. Presently they both fell nodding, and in their dreams wandered away to the green fields of Erin, living over again in their visions the days of their vanished youth.

Now that there was no immediate need for action, Mrs. M'Carty gathered the little Ellen in her arms and sank down on a stool behind the stove. And as she sat there Memory came and stood by her and pointed back to other and happier Christmas Eves when she and Michael had made many a plan to delight the hearts of their numerous brood. The plans were simple enough, to be sure, but the children were too healthily happy to be critical. She recalled the rare Christmas Day when turkey had graced their board, and Michael, in Sunday attire, had sat at the head of the table and labored manfully with the unfamiliar joints of the holiday bird.

"And now," her thought coming back to the present, "I've nothing for them children, barring the matter of a stick of candy that's hardly worth the mentioning, and for the Christmas eatings I've nought but a handful of apples the grocer gave Katy the morning, and a few potatoes, scarce enough for two apiece. And winter that long and dreary, and just my two hands to earn the bread to keep the souls in the whole of us. Oh, worra, worra, whatever shall I do without my Michael?" and Bridget, feeling herself practically alone, for Grandad and Granny still slumbered peacefully, gave vent to her feelings in a heavy sigh. The sound, however, was loud enough to rouse Grandad, who, in his assumed office of comforter-in-general to the M'Carty family, was ever on the alert to perform his duties. He leaned forward and looked anxiously into Bridget's face.

"Biddy, darling," he cried, "sure ye're not grievin' on the blessid Christmas Eve? It's hard for yez with Michael dead an' gone, but grievin' won't bring him back. Think of them that ye have left, — them fine childers, an' Granny there. An' ye've me, but the saints know ye're betther off withoot me, that am just a care to yez and that lame I can't even lift a finger to help yez."

"Now Grandad," cried Bridget, "it's I that am ashamed of you, I am, you that are a comfort, every minit, and no care to be speaking about. And I wasn't forgetting the children, either. They do be plenty of care, so they do, but they give a body a deal of comfort, and not a finger of them could I spare. And Granny there, sure she does be a bit cross now and then along with her rheumatism, but it keeps a body from thinking of worse things when she do be telling the faults of us. And when she's sleeping so sweet-like as she do be now, she's never a bit of care or worry. No, Daddy, it was of my hard work I was thinking, and wondering how I'd get enough to keep us alive this freezing winter."

"Troth, now listen, Biddy!" said Grandad, ready with his word of cheer. "I was just afther dreamin' of a red hen, an' whenever I dream of a red hen, it's good news I'm soon hearin'."

Granny awoke just in time to hear the last sentence.

"Is it a hen ye dreamed ye were?" she queried. "It's because of eatin' that stuff that's not good for the hens, that gave yez them bad dreams."

Then another phase of the cereal question presenting itself she turned to Mrs. M'Carty.

"Bridget M'Carty, is it them same hen aitin's ye're givin' us for our dinner the morrow? Tell me that now?"

So unexpectedly questioned as to her resources for the morrow's provisions, Bridget was startled into the admission that there was nothing in store save a few potatoes and the gift of apples; and the apples, like most gifts to the poor, could not be inspected too closely.

"And it's all from my never getting pay for my washing. Not a penny did they give Katy, and me telling her to wait. Whatever they do be thinking a poor woman is washing their clothes for I do'no. To keep her hands red and sore, and her back just breaking with the bending over the tub, belike. I was to be getting two dollars, and now they'll be waiting till after Christmas to pay, and it's us will be waiting till after Christmas to eat. Sure it's just nothing we have to expect for our Christmas dinner, bedad."

"Well, there now, honey," said Grandad Rafferty, undismayed at the prospect of a dinnerless day. "We'll never mind all that, for them that's expectin' nothin' will never have disappointment to be mournin'."

Granny M'Carty, on hearing Bridget's recital broke forth into genuine Irish lamentations such as she had not indulged in since the news of Michael's untimely death, her wailings interspersed with the most direful prophecies of what was in store for the family.

Fifth Episode

HERR BAUMGÄRTNER'S ESTABLISHMENT SEVEN-THIRTY ON CHRISTMAS EVE

IT had been a very busy day in the Baumgärtner bakery, and now as the old Dutch clock on the wall struck seven, the clerks were flying hither and thither, wrapping up packages and plumping them into baskets, trying to get everything on their last loads, and at the same time to give polite service to the many customers coming and going.

The Christmas puddings had not yet been delivered, but reposed in all their fruity richness on the white-covered table in the rear of the store, and exhaled such delicious odors that the whole air was permeated with what seemed the very essence of Christmas.

The door opened, and this time Katrina Baumgärtner entered. In spite of the rush of business all the clerks stopped long enough to look at Miss Katrina, who had a smile and a "Merry Christmas!" for each. They felt very kindly toward the bright girl who took such an interest in their families; who remembered to ask after Mrs. Reiman's asthma, and Grandfather Potter's rheumatism, and who often sent delicacies to their invalids.

"I forgot all about the cake for the Widow M'Carty's children," she explained, "so I came early to get it. I will mark it, and you won't forget to see that it is delivered, will you?" she asked, beaming on all the clerks at once.

Every clerk declared that Mrs. M'Carty should have her Christmas cake if it had to be taken to her in person.

"Katrina, stay here one leetle while and help your Vater," said the baker as Katrina stopped before his desk, where he was busy making entries in a large ledger. "You vos joost in time. Dere is dose puddings. Wrap dem in dose papers and set dem on dot table by der door oudt. Hans Kleinhardt comes soon mit der cards. Den he takes dose puddings and sends dem away."

"Oh, father," cried Katrina in dismay, "I haven't time. I just came down to get the cake for the Widow M'Carty's children, and the sleigh-ride party will call for me here in a few minutes. Couldn't one of the clerks do it?"

"Nein, nein, Katrina, dose clerks have too much business already. If you vants dot cake for dose M'Cartys, den you wrop up dose puddings right away queek. No vork, no play, mein Katrina."

Katrina slipped off her cloak and went to work. The first pudding had been wrapped up when the sound of bells was heard mingled with the shouts of happy voices. She hastened to the door, but found it was not her sleigh-ride party after all, and was returning to her task when she remembered the cake for the Widow. Selecting a round loaf with nuts and candied fruits dotted over the frosted surface, she took it back with her to the table, did it up, and set it on the shelf behind her. Taking a card, she wrote:

"To Mrs. Michael M'Carty

with a Merry Christmas

from

Katrina Baumgärtner,"

and was about to place it on the cake when another jingle of bells was heard. Catching up the pudding, she hurried again to the front of the store, set the pudding on the table, and, unwittingly, dropped beside it the card bearing the Widow M'Carty's name. She opened the door, but the sleigh with its merry load passed on, and Katrina returned to her enforced labors.

Max Schaub was collecting the last parcels for his load when he chanced to see the package on the table. He picked up the card and read,—"Mrs. Michael M'Carty."

"Bless her sweet eyes,"—meaning Katrina, not the widow,—"'Tis I will see that this cake gets to the Widow M'Carty's children. Does she not ask after the leg of my lame August as if it were her very own,"—meaning Katrina, not the widow,—"and in my coat pocket have I not the singing-box she has sent him for Christmas,—and she with nine small kinder, too?"—meaning the widow, not Katrina.

Thus soliloquizing, he marked a basket in which he deposited the pudding, and gave it to his driver, telling him to leave it at the widow's on the way back to the store.

Katrina tied up the second pudding and placed it on the table from which the first had been removed just as Clerk Reiman entered the door. Remembering Katrina's request, he went to the table, and reading the card, concluded that the package beside it contained the cake destined to make happy the nine small children of the Widow M'Carty. He put it in a basket, marked it for the widow, and gave it to his special driver, who was just starting off with his load.

Katrina's mind was on the anticipated joys of the evening, and she performed her task mechanically, thinking all the time of Johann and longing for the arrival of the sleighing party.

Ten more puddings were enveloped in their wrappings of lace-edged tissue paper; ten more puddings were deposited, one by one, on the table in the front of the store; ten more clerks, seeing the card beside a package,—for each in his hurry forgot to drop the card in his basket,— consigned a pudding to the care of his own driver, charging him to deliver it, without fail, to the Widow M'Carty with a "Merry Christmas from Katrina Baumgärtner."

Katrina had wrapped up the last pudding, when the sound of a horn, a chorus of voices, and the music of sleigh-bells caused her to run to the door once more. She opened it to come face to face with the gallant Johann. Joyfully donning her wraps, she hastened away to join the sleighing party, leaving the thirteenth pudding to its fate.

A few moments later the baker came out of his office, and seeing the puddings gone, nodded his head with satisfaction and said:

"Dot Hans was one goot man. Him I haf nefer to vatch. He does joost vot I tells him, effery time already."

But where was the faithful Hans Kleinhardt who was personally responsible for the safe delivery of those thirteen puddings?

His supper finished, Hans was hastening back to the store with the important cards in his pocket. A shout, a scurrying to avoid a runaway horse, a hurt man, a crowd, an ambulance,—and Hans Kleinhardt, unconscious of all around him, was on his way to the City Hospital.

An hour later a surgeon, with an air of satisfaction, said to a quiet little nurse:

"A beautiful fracture,—compound,—man in good condition,—will recover nicely,—but don't let him talk for twenty-four hours."

And in that man's pocket lay thirteen cards, and they never said a word.

Sixth Episode

WIDOW M'CARTY'S ABODE EIGHT O'CLOCK CHRISTMAS EVE

EVERY ill known or imagined by the pessimistic Granny had been voiced in graphic predictions, but at last even her vocabulary of grumblings was exhausted, and she hobbled off to her pallet, — the thump, thump, thump of her cane beating a resentful retreat.

Grandad still sat in his corner, and Bridget left her uncomfortable seat and dropped into Granny's vacant chair.

"Sure, it ain't much like Christmas Eve I'm thinkin'," she said, glancing at Grandad. "There's the difference in the look of things since Mike, me darling, is gone — him that always went into town, when he stayed home the day before Christmas, to buy presents for me an' the childer. I remimber, yes, I do, 'cause I aint forgot it yet, the elligant bonnit he bought me wanst. What with feathers standing this way an' that, I was the fine lady of all Fifth Street."

"Ye wor that," answered Grandad, looking up with a twinkle in his kind gray eyes. "Ye wor that, Bridget, me girl, an' ye're the same this day, fithers or no fithers."

"It's the feathers makes the bird, Daddy," sighed Bridget, but his pleasant word softened the despairing look on her care-worn face.

"Fithers makes the birds, did ye say, Bridget?" continued Grandad. "What kind of rasonin' is that, sure? Nivir a fither have I seen that was not projuced by wan bird or anither. An' what difference does it make what kind of fithers a bird has whin he's picked, tell me that? For me taste, a bird is betther withoot fithers at all, at all."

"Ah, well," said Bridget, "it's you that have the cheery word, Grandad, and it's good to hear, but to-night I'm that beat out I couldn't throw a stick at Dooley if he came to the door this minit." Mrs. M'Carty looked about the room, so scant with furniture and so cheerless.

"It's no use trying—" she began, but at that moment a knock that fairly rattled the whole shanty called her to the door. It also woke up Granny

31

M'Carty, who thrust her head from the bedclothes and peered into the kitchen.

"'Tis a mistake," she growled as a round package was handed to her daughter, and a strange voice said:

"A Merry Christmas from Katrina Baumgärtner!"

"'Tis a mistake, I say," she continued, as the delivery boy disappeared in the darkness, and Mrs. M'Carty, with hands trembling from excitement, carried the mysterious package to the lean-to.

"Indeed, then, and it's no mistake," she whispered to herself as she opened the package and disclosed to view a beautiful Christmas pudding. "It's Miss Katrina, the darling, that's remembered us this night. One, two, three," she counted, as in imagination she divided the gift among the little M'Cartys. "Four, five, six, — sure, I must be more sparing of my pieces, — but bless the sweet Ellen, she can't eat any, and I'm not needing any myself, — but Grandad, and Granny, they must have a bit; — seven, eight, nine, — it's a trifle small, to be sure, but enough for a taste for the darlings. If Granny hadn't heard the boy, what a fine surprise I'd have for her; but she'll be wanting to know what the likes of me is getting for Christmas. She's that curious, she sleeps with her other eye open just to be seeing what she can hear. But I'll be letting her think it was a mistake, so I will."

Bang! whack! bang! another thundering noise shook the rickety door.

"I told you it was a mistake," screamed Granny. "He's come to take it away from yez."

Mrs. M'Carty's heart sank. The gift evidently was a mistake. Concealing the pudding, divested of its wrappings, under her apron, she hastened to the door, to be handed another package with the same Christmas greeting from Miss Katrina Baumgärtner.

Quick-witted and anxious to deceive the keen eyes and ears of old Granny, she placed both puddings in her apron, and with an audible sigh and lament that "poor folks couldn't have even the things that was give to them," she returned with renewed pleasure to her problem in division.

"Sure," said she, "I must begin my count all over. It's Miss Katrina, bless her sweet eyes, knew one pudding for eleven of us would be just a bite. Now it's two puddings for eleven of us. I wish I had a yardstick and a 'rithmetic to measure them, so I do.

"It's Christmas Eve after all," she continued, regarding with pleasure the two plump puddings, but the sound of approaching footsteps caused her to start again in fear that it might be as Granny had prophesied, all a mistake. She slipped quietly to the door and reached it in time to avert the knock which might have aroused Granny from her dozing.

"A Merry Christmas from Katrina Baumgärtner," shouted a jolly boy as he placed a package in Mrs. M'Carty's hands. There was no mistaking this greeting, nor the contents of the parcel.

"How many be she a-sending?" she whispered cautiously, and added by way of explanation, "The darlings is asleep, and I wouldn't want them to be knowing what a fine Christmas is coming for them."

"Vell, vell, ain'dt one enough?" laughed the boy as he disappeared puddingless, leaving the bewildered Mrs. M'Carty in possession of the third treasure.

"Now Grandad is nodding, and it's meself that's thinking there's no telling how many more Santa Clauses is coming to the M'Carty roof this night. I'll just take the light into the lean-to, and busy myself with a few pieces to fold down for my ironing; and if any more presents do be coming, they'll be taking them to the other door. Then Granny won't be hearing what's going on at all, at all."

The removal of the light proved a wise precaution, though done in innocence of the avalanche of puddings which was fatefully descending upon the M'Carty household.

Greater and greater was the surprise of the widow as pudding after pudding, and pudding after pudding was handed in, until twelve goodly brown concoctions graced her impromptu table,—a long white ironing-board.

"Sure, I'm that excited, I'm fit to tie up," laughed Mrs. M'Carty, as she viewed the bounty of the unsuspecting Katrina. "Twelve puddings for twelve of us, even one for little Ellen. It ain't such a sum as I minded. Blessings on Miss Katrina,—may the saints have her in their keeping,—we've a pudding apiece this Christmas. It's thankful I am, and I'm not complaining, but I could' a' wished she'd tried a little variety. Bedad, if there wasn't so many of them, they'd seem to be more, so they would."

HERR BAUMGÄRTNER'S ESTABLISHMENT TEN O'CLOCK ON CHRISTMAS EVE

IT was ten o'clock on Christmas Eve, and had it not been for the holiday decorations, Baker Baumgärtner's establishment would have presented a somewhat forlorn appearance. The shelves, which earlier in the day were filled with bread, cakes, and confections of all kinds, were now almost bereft of their store, and the whole aspect of the place was disorderly and confused. Boxes and baskets, papers and strings cluttered every available corner. The clerks and drivers, congratulating themselves that they were finishing so early in the evening, had just begun the task of clearing up, when the baker entered the store.

"Donnerwetter!" he exclaimed, on seeing the untidy interior. "Vat a looking place is dis! Oh, vell, I tink I can stand it ven it fills my pockets mit moneys."

He stepped behind the brass screen that kept possible intruders at a respectful distance from the money-drawer. Opening it, he found that the contents of the drawer had grown very perceptibly during his absence, and he surveyed his gains with a feeling of deep self-gratulation.

The Widow M'Carty's cake and the thirteen puddings must have been bread cast upon the waters that day, and so rich was the quality it had returned at once, many fold.

"Der Widow M'Carty's cake, and der orphans' t'ings were nodings," he soliloquized. "But dose puddings! Dere was gut rich stuff in dose, but I got plenty moneys, I can spare dose puddings to my customers ven I gets dem back sometime all right."

Looking through his change window, he saw his clerks, who evidently had made their employer's interests their own, busily rearranging everything before going home, and transforming the chaotic condition of the store into one of order. The fact of their fidelity was very manifest, and may have reminded him of all the pleasures of Christmas Eve which they had forfeited in consequence of his extra holiday trade. According to his custom, he must bestow on each a Christmas remembrance, but it was not in the spirit of a cheerful giver that he contemplated the act.

"Himmel!" he said under his breath. "Twelve clerks and twelve drivers, and Hans Kleinhardt, my head man, besides all dose bakers. It makes me poor ven I am joost rich," and he sighed regretfully at the thought.

The widow's cake and the thirteen puddings, although his voluntary gift, had not been spared without a wrench, and now to be confronted with the necessity of adding to them was too much for human nature, — or at least for Baumgärtner nature. He turned as if addressing some one over his shoulder, — probably his good angel, whose winged company is especially active on Christmas Eve, — and muttered reproachfully, "You expect me to be one Santa Claus again?"

However, he knew that he could not escape his kind intent, and being withal a just man, yielded with a sigh.

From the money-drawer he took a crisp five-dollar bill, laid it on the desk before him, and regarded it thoughtfully. The longer he looked at it the harder it seemed to part with twenty-four of them, and with an emphatic shake of the head he thrust it back again. He next selected a bright silver dollar, but, true to his better nature, he acknowledged its insufficiency, and swept it after the five-dollar bill. His third move was a compromise. He took twenty-four two-dollar bills, looked at them for a moment regretfully, then gathered them in his hand and walked toward where the clerks were just finishing and locking up for the night.

As he passed through the store, he glanced here and there with the keen eye of the master, stopping suddenly as he espied a package which looked suspiciously like a Christmas pudding. A sniff and a touch was enough to satisfy this expert. Down, down deep in his pocket went the precious bills, while the air reverberated with German expletives.

"Gott in Himmel! Donner und Blitzen!" he thundered in tones that had not been heard in that store since the baker had discovered salt instead of sugar on a large batch of cinnamon kuchen.

The alarmed clerks stared at the baker in consternation. Two or three of the new ones retreated to the door, but the braver hurried to their irate employer, who stood glowering like a thunder-cloud and pointing to a certain round object reposing innocently on a table.

"Der Teufel! Was meint das? Das geht nicht," shrieked the baker, who was apt, under excitement, to fall into his native tongue. "Who has not his pudding got? Wo ist dat Hans Kleinhardt?"

The head clerk could not be found, and as none of the other clerks knew aught of the Christmas pudding scheme, the direst misunderstanding ensued. In the midst of the excitement the front door opened and Katrina rushed in, her cheeks aglow and her enthusiasm beautiful to behold were there no puddings in the case.

"Oh, Father, I ran in—" she began, then stopped suddenly. A glance at her father told her that some dreadful thing had happened to disturb the peaceful serenity that usually pervaded Herr Baumgärtner's establishment. The baker turned to her.

"Vat did you do mit dose Christmas puddings, already?"

"Why, Father," answered Katrina, "I wrapped them up and put them on the table by the door, just as you told me to, before I went to the sleigh-ride. They must be here somewhere."

A vigorous search for the puddings ensued, but it was a fruitless quest.

After a little, when the baker had calmed down somewhat, Katrina ventured to tell her errand.

"I came in to see if the Widow M'Carty's cake had been sent to her, and if it hasn't, the sleigh-ride party is here and we will drive down and take it to her."

"Dat cake? I know nodings about it. Did any von send the Widow M'Carty her cake?" turning to the clerks.

"The Widow M'Carty's cake!" cried all the clerks in unison. "Why, I sent it to her!"

"The Widow M'Carty's cake!" chorused twelve highly excited drivers. "Why, I took it to her!"

"Mein Gott! Mein Gott!" ejaculated the baker as the fate of his puddings dawned upon him. "Twelve cakes to the Widow M'Carty, und day was all puddings!"

Eighth Episode

WIDOW M'CARTY'S ABODE TEN-O'CLOCK ON CHRISTMAS EVE

GREAT is the mission of the plum pudding to elevate and refine. Poor Mrs. M'Carty, who had been too tired even to throw a stick at the Dooleys, and had meant only to wait for the return of the children to seek her much-shared bed, now began to bethink herself of active preparations for the unexpected festivities of the morrow.

The fire was encouraged to bestir itself, a kettle of water was put on to heat, and pails and scrubbing-brush were brought from the lean-to.

At this juncture the returned sightseers burst into the room, Katy and Norah both talking at once. Terence and Denny were not far behind in their utterances, and though perhaps more coherent, were certainly not less enthusiastic. It was well that the eloquence of tongues spoke in their wonder-filled eyes, for otherwise no mere mortal could have interpreted the steadily rising tones and varied inflections which were excitedly mingled in a Babel of sounds.

The scraping of snow and the confusion attendant upon their sudden entrance filled Mrs. M'Carty with new alarm, but she collected her wits enough to whisper with desperate vehemence, while she waved her scrubbing-cloth wildly:

"Whist now, will you, and mind that I don't hear another word out of your heads, or you'll be waking up Granny, for upon my soul, her eyes ain't been shut more than this blessed two minutes. I hope to goodness you won't be disturbing her, for I be just going to do up her cap for the Christmas. Now off with yourselves to bed, and not another word out of your heads to-night, till to-morrow. Och, Katy dear! What would you be telling me that for again? Sure you've repeated it three times, not counting the twice of Terence's. Now, now, boys, will you mind your mother, and go to bed like good children, and be getting up bright and early with Christmas morning faces on you?"

The boys obeyed and were soon deep in dreams in which "cops" were selling newspapers out in the cold, and newsboys were in Huyler's warming their feet while ladies in fluffy furs treated them to candy and ice-cream.

The widow bestowed a grateful look on the two lads asleep in the bunk which had been built in the little jog between the kitchen and lean-to. Then she tiptoed past them into the inner room where she found Katy and Norah whispering excitedly and with no prospect of cessation until their mother's voice reminded them of their promise to be quiet.

"Now, child of grace, get into the bed," she said to Katy, "and don't be keeping yourselves awake till the morning, and don't be forgetting to say your prayers."

Mrs. M'Carty slipped back to the kitchen, where Grandad sat dozing in his one-armed rocking-chair, and immediately began to busy herself with fresh energy.

"Off with your shirt, Grandad," she said, cheerfully, as the old man gave a sleepy jerk to his head. "It's the best one you have, and I'll wash it out in a minute and iron it to-night. You can wrap that old shawl about you, and while your shirt's a-soaking, I'll give you a brush over with a bit of soap and water, for it'll be that lively in the morning, there'll never be the bit of a chance, at all; and I'm not one to leave till the proper time them things I've the opportunity of doing now."

The shirt being consigned to the soaking process, Bridget next attacked her father. When his ablutions were finished, she pinned a shawl around his shoulders, and moved his chair nearer the fire. With his cheeks glowing from their recent administration of soap and water, Grandad watched the washing and starching of his blue gingham shirt, thinking the while of its stiffness, which would encase him on the morrow, but at the same time regarding it as one of those trials to be borne without complaint.

Mrs. M'Carty hung the shirt close to the fire to dry, while she "scrubbed thot strip in front of the sthove;" then she left the strip, "bekase," as she said in her state of bewilderment and joy, "Oi musht do the shirt whiles the irons is hot, an' it do beat all how fasht thim irons does het oop whin ye ain't waitin' on thim." So, getting up from her knees, and leaving a good-sized puddle for future attention, she proceeded to pound the iron on Grandad's shirt and one neck-cloth, turning now and then to the sweet-tempered old man, who sat smiling at her as she bustled to and fro.

"Ye'll be that fine to-morrow," said Bridget, "that you'll not be after knowing yourself, sure. And your hair will be combed that smooth, you'll look ten years younger. It does be, I mind, it's the hair that adds the years to your life."

Grandad Rafferty, his spirits undepressed by what sufferings the ordeal of starch and comb might have in store for him, tapped his empty pipe on the edge of the stove and responded softly,—

"'Tis ye, Biddy M'Carty, would hearten up a ghost, so ye would."

"It's a quare way ye have of jabberin' all through the night that a body can't get a wink of slape," came the querulous tones of Granny from her pallet in the farther corner of the inner room. "An' it's that cold in here—an' why in the world do ye be burnin' the fire in the night an' wasthin' the wood, an' we'll be sittin' 'round freezin' to-morra with no fire at all,—so we will."

For a moment Bridget's spirits fell, but the next instant they rose again.

"Wait a bit, now, Granny, and I'll be bringing you a warm iron to your feet, and before you know it you'll be dreaming of the smell of fresh peat coming in the door."

"Dhramin' is it, Oi'd be?" growled Granny, and in a moment more her cane was heard thumping vigorously on the floor. Bridget and Grandad had scarcely more than time to exchange a sympathetic glance when Granny appeared with her red flannel petticoat over her nightgown and a black and white shawl wrapped around her shoulders. She came hobbling in, sniffing the sudsy moisture and complaining:

"It's more roometiz for me, so it is.—Begorra, but it's piercin' cold in there.—It's you that has the comfortable spot, Misther Rafferty. It do be that draughty when yer comin' through this way," and thus speaking her mind on a few points, Granny made her way slowly to her chair and seated herself in it.

Meantime Bridget was quietly raising geysers of suds in her endeavors to conceal the luckless cap.

"Bridget M'Carty," demanded Granny, "what on earth do ye be workin' at there that ye be puttin' out me eyes fairly, with splashin' soapsuds in them? Is it my cap yer sousin' up and down, now? Indade, then, and it is, an' me just wantin' it. No wonder I'll be gettin' more pain in my bones, with the wind blowin' like a penethratin' blast through the windy, an' me with no cap, an' ye kapin' yerself warm be exercisin'."

"Och, now, Granny," said Bridget, hoping to pacify her, "sure I thought it would be a grand surprise for you when you woke in the morning, to see them tie-ends hanging before your eyes all starched up, that Miss Barney's mother might just be envying you."

"Envyin' me, would she?" replied Granny. "Like enough 'twill not be dry by mornin' at all, an' whin I do put it on, I'll be gettin' that pain in me head agin."

Grandad's conciliatory remark was never heard, for Granny's mutterings continued while her patient daughter-in-law starched and ironed the cap. When it was finished and hung by the fire to air, Bridget, with a weary smile, turned to her father.

"Come now, Daddy," she said, "you'll not be wanting to get up if you don't be getting to your bed soon."

"Well, thin, if ye're meanin' to put the light out in me face, I'll go back to my bed before ye do," snapped Granny, and so she went.

When Grandad had been snugly tucked into his cot in the kitchen, and the pails and mops put out of sight, Bridget lay down to a well-earned sleep and dreamed that the fairies were pelting her with puddings, every third one of which fell into her mouth and was swallowed whole.

Ninth Episode

HERR BAUMGÄRTNER'S ESTABLISHMENT CHRISTMAS DAY

HERR Baumgärtner's first impulse, on finding out what had become of his Christmas puddings, was to send at once to the Widow M'Carty's and have them returned to him. Had it not been for the lateness of the hour, doubtless this is what would have happened.

But the night brings counsel, even in the matter of plum puddings, and by morning the baker had concluded that it was wiser to let the unlucky gifts remain in their misfit quarters. Perhaps Katrina's remark, that his customers would be wroth if they found they had eaten puddings that had been stored for a night, even, in so well-inhabited an abode, influenced his decision.

However that may be, the baker said to Katrina as he sat down to his breakfast:

"Vell, Katrina, if we haf given somedings away in the wrong place, we will not now take it back. But Katrina, dose beautiful puddings, and dose M'Cartys! ach! ach!" and he shook his head sorrowfully at the thought that these culinary triumphs should have fallen to those so incapable of appreciating a wonderful Baumgärtner plum pudding.

In the eyes of the baker, to give twelve Christmas puddings to the M'Cartys was indeed to cast one's pearls before swine.

Herr Baumgärtner could not remain out of sorts for any length of time, and when he found by his plate a gift from his beloved Katrina of a long meerschaum pipe from the Fatherland, he smiled and said:

"Ven I smokes dat pipe den I forget dose plum puddings."

The pipe, indeed, performed a placatory mission, for as the first rings of its smoke curled upward, it became a veritable pipe of peace.

Later the baker and Katrina attended church together, and at the close of the service Herr Baumgärtner left his daughter and wended his way to the bakery.

He tarried in front of the window occupied by the Christmas tree, whose gaily trimmed branches recalled to him so vividly the years when his little Fritz had furnished the joy and merriment of the holiday season. How the wee baby had bounded,—almost out of his mother's arms,—at sight of his first tree! Now the baker had only Katrina to cheer him, while he, in turn, was devoted to his daughter. His present errand to the bakery was to get some of her favorite Marzipan for their Christmas dinner, it having slipped his mind the night before in the distraction of the pudding calamity.

As he unlocked the door and entered the store, almost the first object to claim his attention was the last Christmas pudding "left standing alone; all its nut-brown companions labelled and gone." None of his clerks had dared to risk his position by meddling with that package. Herr Baumgärtner picked up the package, saying with a sigh, as he unwrapped it:

"Oh, well, you might as well go in the window and make a good show. Maybe I can sell you for New Year's day."

While the baker was busy arranging his wares to make room for the pudding, a man came sauntering slowly up the street, pausing as he came to the window. He was clad in a rough suit which here and there showed the want of a prudent feminine stitch. The first glance showed him to be simply an honest Hibernian laborer. Further scrutiny disclosed the fact that he was a man who had passed through unusual experiences, for his bronzed face told of hardship and exposure. At each footfall he looked up imploringly at the passer-by, only to turn away with a sigh of disappointment. As he looked at the good things in the baker's window, he said to himself:

"Ah, my poor Bridget and the little ones are likely fasting, when they ought to be having the fill of the table. And myself looking every place for them till the feet of me is wore off entirely. The cottage is empty, and the priest is a new one, and can't tell me nothing. Mebbe they've gone to the old country, or mebbe they're all—" and here he shuddered and shut his lips tightly, for he would not admit the worst.

"Be jabers," his thoughts taking on a new turn, as he caught sight of a pudding being placed in the window before him, "if I could just find them, wouldn't I make the mouths of them water with that pudding. Like enough Patsy and Maggie and Norah and Katy ain't had a bite to eat of anything decent these six months. Heaven bless the spalpeens, how they would fall on that pudding! And me darling Biddy, bedad, ain't tasted one since she was living with the Church of Ireland minister in Limerick. And here I be, with money enough to buy them everything good, and not one out of them left to be buying for. Oh, well, I've no mind in me to eat myself, but I might as well step in and buy them two buns," and thereupon he entered the store.

The new customer did not look especially promising; still, the baker had known far shabbier individuals to invest a dollar, even, on a holiday, so he advanced with a smile and said:

"Vat can I do for you, my friend?"

Pointing to the large, well-sugared buns, the man began, "Give me two—" when his glance fell upon something white that lay on the counter,—that ubiquitous card that had wrought so much mischief; the card bearing the name and address of Mrs. Michael M'Carty.

"Vat's the matter mit you?" said the baker impatiently, anxious for him to complete his order.

"Oh, my God, what's this?" cried the man, snatching up the card.

"Dot? Vy, dat is one card to go mit one cake to the Widow M'Carty."

"Widdy, widdy, is it?" cried the man, angrily. "Sure the man that calls her that will answer to me for it. Why would she be a widdy, and me working and saving as a respectable husband should for her?"

"Wait awhile,—tell me,—was you Mr. Widow M'Carty?"

"Who would I be then, but Michael M'Carty? It's some of them blathering Barneys that's after calling me Bridget a widdy. Their lying tongues are all the time wagging with some scandal on a woman that hasn't a good strong man to protect her and the childers. But tell me quick, where are they, and are they alive, all alive?"

"I hear my Katrina speak about dem. But vere haf you been this long time? I t'ought you was drownded, already."

"Sure, 'twas meself thought so too, the whole of the night, and I wished I'd never stepped me foot on that old tub of a Go-Between, for it was the devil's own. When we got in Lake Superior, a storm came after us sudden, and we all went down together. I was in a hole of a place I had to slape in, — sure a dog couldn't close his eye in that corner, — and in the middle of the night, down they came hustling every one of us out. 'Say yer prayers,' says they, 'for we're a-goin' to the bottom, and the Lord help us. There's not one of yez will see yer darlints again.' The water was terrible boisterous, and grabbed everythin' off the decks. Faith, it wouldn't have been so bad if we'd a place left for the sole of our foot, but she was gone entirely. A board hit me and I hung on to it, and Pat Sweeny came up from down in the water and hung on with me, and the noises of that night I'll never be getting out of me head. When it come daylight we see the pilot-house a-floating, and we got on that, and Pat Sweeny waved his red handkerchief, and I tried to push us along with the board, to the land we see a long way off. In the middle of the morning, we spied a little boat coming to us, and may the blessed Virgin spare them two men in it as long as they live. It was a bare enough place we come to, but 'twas the land, and may I be struck dead if ever I take me two feet off it, for it's not the likes of me will set foot on one of them traps of the devil again."

"Ach, Gott, das war wundervoll, wundervoll," said the baker, "but tell me vy you stayed so long away?"

"And what would the likes of me be doing with everything gone, but to be getting some money to come with? There were some copper mines there, and Pat and me went digging in the mines, and the engineer dying sudden-like with a fall down the shaft, it was me was there to be getting his job. I wrote Bridget as soon as ever I thought she would be looking for me coming home, and told her I wouldn't be there till I could earn some money to come by land, and what with the fine engineer wages I was getting, she needn't be expecting me till the end of the season. When I came home with me pile of money to give them all a grand Christmas, I found 'em lost on me, and I've looked every place these three days, and never a sound of them have I heard till now, and God bless ye for the good words you're giving me this day. — Troth, now that I'm after finding them, I ought to be buying that grand pudding in the windy," and diving into his pocket, he produced a roll of bills.

"Nein, nein," said the baker, waving the money away, "dat pudding was not made to sell, it was made to gif away. You takes dat pudding to Mrs. M'Carty mit the gompliments of Herr Baumgärtner."

With a hearty Merry Christmas, Michael M'Carty hurried away with the pudding in one hand, and the card in the other. Herr Baumgärtner, taking his Marzipan, went home to tell Katrina the news, laughing over his Christmas joke, and chuckling to himself:

"Dat is vere dat pudding seems to belong!"

Tenth Episode

WIDOW M'CARTY'S ABODE CHRISTMAS DAY

MRS. M'CARTY rose early on Christmas morning, her mind bewildered by the fantastic visions of the night.

"Sure, them puddings was all a dream," she said to herself, as she kindled her fire, "and what's the good of such dreams as that, but just to make a body discouraged with the truth of the daytimes? But, any how, I'll look at where I dreamed I put them, and then my mind will be easy for me work."

More skeptical than hopeful, she went to the place where she had hidden them, and lo! to her great joy there they were,—twelve luscious, fruity puddings.

"And they're just bursting with richness, and begging to be ate," she said. "It'll be a grand day for the childer, and they shall have their fill, for it's many a long, hungry day they'll be seeing before another Christmas."

Breakfast was never a protracted function in the M'Carty household, but to Mrs. M'Carty, who was anxious to begin the festive preparations which the puddings had made possible, the scanty meal seemed unusually prolonged. Nothing but action could keep her from syndicating her secret before the proper moment, so while the repast was in progress, she hurried about doing, undoing, and doing over again, various household tasks. Finally Granny M'Carty, who had noticed Bridget's restlessness, exclaimed:

"Are ye crazy, then, Bridget M'Carty? It's the third time this day ye've spread me bed, and ye'll not lave a whole fither in me pillow with yer senseless beatin's."

"Well," said Mrs. M'Carty, ceasing from her labor, "if you're done with your breakfast, listen to me. Praise to the good Saint Antony, I found a ten-cent piece yesterday, I'd been saving that long I forgot I had it entirely, and with the help of Grandad's two lucky pennies he was never intending to spend,—may the saints spare him long to us,—I've a stick of candy apiece for the whole of you."

"Hoorooh!" shouted all the little McCartys in chorus.

"Blessin's on the good Saint Antony!" said Grandad Rafferty, beaming on the excited children.

"Stop yer sphakin' with such a noise!" cried Granny. "Them racketin's would deafen the saints themselves, so they would."

"Then would them saints be getting ear-trumpets like Tim Barney's grandmother?" queried little Norah, climbing on the back of Granny's chair and peering over her shoulder.

"Go along with yez, an' don't be askin' such irrirevent questions, an' kape yerself from the back of me chair, a-shakin' me roometiz all over me."

Bridget thumped on the table for quiet and proceeded to distribute the sticks of candy, each wrapped in a separate piece of paper. Grandad unrolled the paper and eyed his stick of candy lovingly.

"Troth, it's peppermint," he said, "an' there's nothin' like peppermint to comfort a body's stomick. It's that long since I tasted it, I'd clane forgot how it looked, bedad."

"Well, Bridget M'Carty," said Granny M'Carty, "It's ye that might have minded me health an' remembered that lemin with roometiz is like pourin' ile on fire. Ye must know, if ye have any sense, — which I misdoubt, — that roometiz hates lemin as bad as the devil hates holy wather," and she sniffed contemptuously.

"Never mind that, Granny," said Grandad. "Bridget rolled up them candy and never took note of the kinds, so there'd be no strivin' with the childers. I'll take yer lemin an' ye're welcome to me peppermint. 'Twill warm yer stomick an' yer feelin's, an' acushla machree, it's not so hard on the teeth ayther," and he surrendered his candy with a charming smile.

"Me teeth are as good as yours any day," retorted Granny, but she did not hesitate to make the exchange. However, she inspected the candy carefully and wiped it on the corner of her shawl before applying it to her mouth.

"Now, then," said Mrs. M'Carty, after the candy had disappeared, "listen while I do be telling you the order of the day. You boys, Denny and Terence, slip across to the pile of lumber handy on the tow-path, and bring me back three wide boards. We'll borry them for a table, and take them back when we're done. My family is all going to sit down to once to their Christmas dinner, the same as them rich folks do on the avenue. And there'll be a place for me poor Michael, that was and isn't. Run along now, boys, and pick clean ones, and you, Katy and Norah, wash the dishes, and when the table is fixed you can all go on the avenue and look in the windys, but mind you're home when the bells are ringing for twelve."

Their tasks were quickly finished, and eight little M'Cartys set off for their outing, two-year-old Patsy being bestowed in a box nailed on an old sled, and drawn by the others in turn. Grandad Rafferty watched them until they were out of sight and sound.

"It's a fine time they'll be afther havin'," he said as he took little Ellen on his knee and settled himself comfortably in his chair, — or as comfortably as the unwonted stiffness of shirt and neckcloth would permit. Then he whispered a wonderful story to the baby, and though she could not understand a word, it served its purpose, for presently the little head nodded and the big blue eyes closed in slumber.

Granny M'Carty, who from the inner room had herself been observing the departure of her grandchildren toward the habitations of affluence, now returned to her seat by the fire.

"'Tis I would never let them childer go wanderin' off like that, with a chance of their never comin' home agin," she commented, "but annyhow it'll be sthill for a bit."

The children safely out of the way, Mrs. M'Carty began at once her arrangements for the feature of the day, — the Christmas dinner so bountifully provided with dessert.

She took from her chest her one linen table cloth, woven in a most elaborate design of shamrocks. Her husband had seen and admired the pattern, displayed in a shop window, one St. Patrick's Day, and it being in the first year of his marriage, when there was but Bridget to share his purse, he had bought the cloth and given it to her for a present. The occasions which had been deemed worthy so beautiful a table-cover, had been few and far removed, so the linen was "every bit as good as new."

"You're fine enough for the queen's use," said Mrs. M'Carty, apostrophizing the cloth as she spread it carefully on her improvised dining-table and smoothed its snowy folds. "Sure, you're a trifle small for me big table, so I'll be putting you in the middle, and piecing you out at the two ends with me red and white Sunday table-cloths that ain't seen the daylight since we came to this sorry hole of a place, for it's not oilcloth that the M'Cartys shall be eating their dinner on this day."

The linen cloth being spread in the centre of the table and supplemented at either end with a "red Sunday table-cloth" of more prosperous days, Mrs. M'Carty took from the top shelf in the cupboard her "set of flowered dishes"—another early marital gift. Though cheap in quality, and the plates, cups, etc., in half-dozens instead of dozens, these dishes had been Mrs. M'Carty's special pride ever since Michael had proudly bestowed them upon her.

"Look, Biddy, me darlint," he had said. "I've brought you as grand a lot of dishes as ever I saw, and do you mind them posies they have? They're like the roses growing forninst Father Kelly's wall, where I used to meet you when you were Biddy Rafferty."

"Go along wid yer foolishness, Michael M'Carty," was Bridget's reply, but she had cherished the gift above all her other possessions, and like the table-cloth, the dishes were used but seldom.

"Bridget M'Carty!" cried Granny, when she saw Bridget setting out the dishes, "are ye usin' them dishes me poor b'y bought with his hard earnin's? I'd think ye'd more respect for Michael than to set out them fine plates to be broken by them careless haythins."

But Bridget assured Granny she would keep watch over the precious ware, and went on with her preparations as zealously as though she were preparing a banquet for noble folk. She had a small package of tea which had been given her by one of the conductors for whom she washed. He wasan Irish boy lately come from the old country, and Mrs. M'Carty's sympathy for his homesickness had won from him this Christmas remembrance. The tea was a most welcome gift, for her finances had not permitted her to buy this beverage for many days. She had not mentioned it, for she wished to have as many surprises as possible, for, thought she, "Surprises is about all they'll be getting."

Granny had followed her daughter-in-law's movements with a lofty, scornful look, but when she saw her take down the old brown teapot and give it a washing, she could not refrain from a question.

"Is it tay ye're afther havin'?" she asked, almost forgetting herself at the thought and speaking in an amiable tone.

"Yes, Granny, but I was intending it for a surprise."

"Wan time is as good as another for a surprise," said Granny. "If it's a good one it gives a body somethin' pleasant to be thinkin' about, an' if it's a bad one, then the sooner ye're told the sooner ye do be gettin' over it."

The animated look in Granny's eyes showed that, in her opinion, this surprise was a good one, and Grandad Rafferty opened his eyes in astonishment when he heard her crooning a bit of the "Low-backed Car."

"It's the peppermint did it," said he to himself, "an' may the saints kape it lastin' till bedtime."

By noon the banqueting-hall of the M'Cartys presented a most festal appearance. The flowered dishes were displayed to the best advantage, and the red cotton table-cloths served the purpose of a color scheme. The baked apples adorned the centre of the table, flanked at either side by plates of bread. The oven door stood ajar, disclosing two dishes of steaming potatoes waiting to be transferred to the table, and later to the plates and stomachs of the juvenile M'Cartys.

When the twelve o'clock bells began to ring, Bridget poured the water over the tea and set the teapot over the fire, where the beverage immediately began boiling with a vigor that would have appalled an epicurean taste. Granny M'Carty was moved up to the centre of the table on one side, and Grandad Rafferty was installed opposite. Little Ellen, in the charge of her grandfather, immediately preëmpted a spoon, and in her enjoyment of the new plaything brought it down with a smart rap on one of the plates.

"I told yez ye'd be afther havin' ev'ry last one of them dishes broke," scolded Granny. "Ye're that extravagant with yer things, Bridget M'Carty, it's no wonder ye went an' lost yer husband. An' where's them childers that was to be comin' home at twilve? Sure they never do as they're bid unless the devil's afther them, an' if they're not here soon the tay will be sphoiled entirely," and she sniffed the air anxiously.

At this critical moment the door, true to its habit, sprung open, and the eight laughing, panting, ruddy M'Carty heirs and heiresses filled the little room to overflowing. Their wraps were thrown aside and they were about to make a grand rush for the table when Mrs. M'Carty interposed.

"Never in me life have I see worse manners since me eyes had the misfortune to rest on them Dooleys down the tow-path. You're patterns in manners when you're asleep, but where do you keep your decency daytimes? Go to the shed and show yourselves to the water and soap, and don't be keeping me dinner waiting long, either."

Bang, thump, splash, grunt, gurgle, constituted the sign audible of the little M'Cartys' cleansing. The hands and faces were polished, the comb hastily passed round, and in they trooped, this time more quietly, as if they had scrubbed off some of their boisterous spirits.

Norah had found a bit of holly, with which she adorned the dish of baked apples, while Terence, with much effort, pulled from his pocket a package wrapped in pink paper and laid it with an important air on Granny's plate.

"Merry Christmas, with a present for you, Granny," he said.

"What's that you've been buying?" said Mrs. M'Carty, "and you with no money to buy nothing with."

"I didn't buy it," said Terence.

"I'll not have anythin' to do with stholen stuff, ye wicked craytur," exclaimed Granny, pushing the offending package away from her.

"I didn't steal it, neither," said Terence, proudly. "I leave such works for them Dooleys," and he held his head aloft and went over by his mother.

"I believe you, Terence, my boy," said Mrs. M'Carty. "But wherever did you get it?"

"He axed for it," interposed Katy. "We were that cold, and when we came to a drug-store, Terence, says he, 'Let's slip in and get warm and smell all them perfoomery and things.' And the drug-store man says, 'What does we be wanting,' and Terence says, 'We just came in to get warm, but we'd buy something if we had the money.' 'What would you buy?' said the man, and Terence says, 'Perfoomery for my mother, and stuff to cure Granny's roometiz.' 'Is that all ye want?' says the man; 'then get your fingers warm and take these to your mother and Granny, with a merry Christmas.'"

"And here's your perfoomery," cried Terence, handing a smaller pink package to his mother, who exclaimed over it with delight.

"Sure, it's better than flowers, and far more lasting," she said, "and it's glad I am you brought it."

"I can't read this writin' at all, at all. The sphellin' is too small for me eyes," said Granny, once more becoming the centre of interest.

Mrs. M'Carty took the bottle and read aloud the directions.

"And you're to take a teaspoonful after each meal," she concluded.

"Humph!" snorted Granny. "An' does that drug-store man lay out to furnish me with the meals? I'd like to be told that now. Me that hasn't had a decint bit since ye let me poor Michael go off and get drownded in the cold wather."

The clatter attendant on the seating of the children at the table prevented the latter part of Granny's speech from being heard. The smaller M'Cartys were placed either side of Grandad, the older ones being seated by Granny. The potatoes were transferred to the board, and Mrs. M'Carty, taking the little Ellen, sat down at the nominal foot of the table, opposite the empty place set in memory of her husband. For awhile naught was spoken save only the few occasional words necessary in asking for more food. Bridget sipped a little tea, but the sight of the vacant chair quite destroyed her appetite. She looked thin and care-worn, and very unlike the brave wife who with cheery words had sped her husband on his unlucky voyage.

When the children's appetites were somewhat appeased, their tongues began to fly as they recounted the morning adventures,—the sights, the sounds, and all the little incidents which had gone to make up a happy morning.

Finally Bridget rapped on the table for silence.

"Whist again every last one of you while I make a request. Terence, me lad, slip over to the wood-box and bring whatever you find there. It's for your Grandad."

Terence quickly obeyed, while the others looked on in eager expectance. He returned with a round package wrapped in tissue and lace-trimmed paper and set it before Grandad, who undid it with surprising alacrity.

"May the saints presarve us!" he exclaimed. "If it isn't as fine a puddin' as my old eyes ever see in me life."

"Me, me!" cried little Patsy, "me wants a puddin'."

"Yes, me little Patsy," said Grandad, "ye shall have a bite as soon as my knife can cut it. There now, sit down, all of yez, till I have a chance at it,"—for the children were crowding about the old man to get a glimpse of the beautiful pudding. But before his knife had so much as touched it, Bridget interposed.

"Hold a bit," she said. "Katy, darling, run to the shed and look under the wash-tub and bring the contents to Granny."

Katy fairly flew to the shed and returned bearing aloft a package which in size, shape, and wrappings was identical with that which had just been set before Grandad. Granny opened it, displaying the mate to Grandad's pudding.

"Whee, whee!" cried little Patsy. "Me wants it! Me wants it!"

But Bridget was ready with a third order.

"Norah, my jewel, you'll likely find something to your credit forninst the dishpan."

Norah lifted the dishpan and in a trice pudding number three was standing beside its predecessors.

"I'll bet yer, kids," said Terence, the ready spokesman, "there's a pudding for every last one of us. Let's get busy and hunt. Sure, I see something under the stove."

Mrs. M'Carty let them hunt. They preferred this, and the fun ran high as one pudding after another was discovered. The house, though so small, held more hiding-places than one would have supposed, and it was some time before the last pudding consented to be found. Mrs. M'Carty allowed each one to cut his pudding and eat a generous portion. To more fastidious palates, cold plum pudding without sauce might have seemed a doubtful luxury, but to the little M'Cartys, who never before had tasted the dainty, the plum puddings were a veritable "feast of Lucullus." Baby Ellen was given a crumb or two, and she goo-ed, and gurgled, and smiled on them all as if she thought herself the cause of all this festivity.

"Praise the blessid saints," said Grandad, "they didn't forget us this Christmas day, an' these are grand puddin's."

"Grand indade," replied Granny. "If Bridget M'Carty had said her prayers proper-like, it's other things besides puddin's she would have asked the saints for, but she's that foolish, she can't keep two words in her head to once. When she thinks puddin's, she just thinks puddin's, an' not aven the sauce, bedad."

"Annyhow, Granny, ye must say it was fine puddin's she did be thinkin'."

"Av course they're fine, but there's nothin' but puddin's, an' I have to ate them or be stharvin', I expect," and Granny helped herself to the third piece and passed her cup to Bridget to be filled the fourth time.

While the puddings were being eaten Mrs. M'Carty told the tale of the mysterious presents. So dramatic was her exposition of the twelve knocks that had been the precursors of the twelve puddings that when, as she finished, there came a loud and emphatic knock at the door, Grandad Rafferty, his mind on Bridget's story, ejaculated:

"Another puddin'!"

"Annuzzer puddin'!" lisped little Patsy.

"May the saints forgit to sind us another puddin'!" said Granny M'Carty.

Before any one had thought to open the door, it opened from without, and there stood, looking in at the group, a tall, haggard, weary man.

"Holy Virgin save us, it's Michael's ghost!" cried Granny, covering her face with her hands.

For a full minute the inmates of the shanty and the man at the door stared at each other. Then Mrs. M'Carty heard the one word:

"Bridget!"

It was enough. Quite forgetting little Ellen, who tumbled unceremoniously to the floor, Mrs. M'Carty sprang from her chair.

"It's no ghost! It's no ghost!" she cried, sobbing and laughing. "It's my Michael,—my heart of the world,—my Michael,—come back from the dead," and she threw herself into his arms.

Exclamations and explanations were now the order of the day. Mrs. M'Carty in her Christmas lavishness had used all of the tea, but she reheated the contents of the teapot and cut a slice of pudding for her husband, but Michael, established in his erstwhile empty place at the table, was too happy for either eating or drinking.

The dinner lasted as long as did that of any of "swelldom's four hundred," for one cannot relate in a few moments the happenings of months, nor can so wonderful a gift as that of Katrina Baumgärtner be passed over with a few words.

When the tale of the puddings was ended Michael, with a merry twinkle in his eye, said to Norah:

"Norah, my jewel, be lookin' outside the door there, and see what you can be after findin'."

Eight little M'Cartys ran to the door. A scramble, a noisy return, and down on the table descended the thirteenth pudding.

At dusk Granny M'Carty and Grandad Rafferty sat in their accustomed places by the fire. Baby Ellen was fast asleep in Grandad's arms. The children were out for a run in the fresh air, and Bridget and Michael were enjoying a few moments of happy converse together in the lean-to.

Grandad rocked gently to and fro, nodding and smiling to himself as if his thoughts were very pleasant company. The sight of his cheerful face, dimly seen by the small lamp, was too much for Granny.

"It's meself," she began, "as can sit here with never a soul to be shpakin' to me, an' ev'ry one of me bones and nerves achin' with the excitemint of this day; an' it's ye, Misther Rafferty, that can sit there grinnin' and noddin' like a crazy loon. It's them that has a fine consait of themselves that getsalong in this world, I mind. An' look at them puddin's, — "

"Puddin's? Puddin's?" said Grandad, rousing from his reverie and looking about as if he expected to see a second installment.

"Yes, puddin's!" mimicked Granny. "What's to be done with the leavin's of them thirteen puddin's, the unlucky things?"

"Mrs. M'Carty, don't be callin' them puddin's unlucky. Sure, 'twas the thirteenth puddin' that let Michael be findin' his lost family. Think no more of them. Remember yer Michael that couldn't sthay lost, an' it's because ye was so lucky to be namin' him afther the good saint. Saint Michael an' the old dragon, ye mind, — "

"An' is it meself ye're afther callin' an old dragon?" almost screamed Granny.

"Indade and indade, Mrs. M'Carty," began Grandad, regretting his unfortunate allusion to the dragon, and anxious to avert the impending tirade, "I'm not callin' ye an old dragon, at all, at all. It's — it's yer roometiz I mane. Yes, sure, it's that is the old dragon, an' Michael will fight it for yez, an' I know he'll conquer it entirely, just as sure as I know there was luck in them thirteen puddin's. An' Granny," he went on, growing still more

Utopian in his predictions, "ye'll soon be walkin' 'round gay as a cricket, with never an ache or a pain to be throublin' yez."

"Are ye sure of all that, Misther Rafferty?" asked Granny eagerly. Grandad had conjured up too blissful a vision for even her gloomy spirits to withstand.

"Sure? Av course I'm sure!" answered Grandad promptly, and pounded his chair with emphasis. "It's as good as done this minit, an' there's such good times comin' for all of us, it's not aven the quane we'll be envyin'."

Granny sat for a few moments in silence. Then she turned to Grandad.

"An' did ye mind, Misther Rafferty," she said with a little brightness, "did ye mind, I say, that Michael had the gold ring on his finger?"

"I did that," answered Grandad. "Me two eyes took sight of it as soon as ever he sthirred his hand, an' it was shinin' as bright as ever it was before he went an' got drownded. An' that's another sign of good times comin' for us. An' listen, Mrs. M'Carty, it's for yer Michael bein' ev'ry bit as good as gold himself, that them saints went to all the throuble of undrownding him an' bringin' him back to us that nades him."

And for once Granny smilingly agreed.

THE END.